Jasper's Beanstalk

Nick Butterworth and Mick Inkpen

Hodder
Children's
Books

On Monday
Jasper found
a bean.

On Tuesday
he planted it.

On Wednesday he watered it.

On Thursday
he dug and raked
and sprayed and
hoed it.

On Friday night he picked

up all the slugs and snails.

On Saturday he even mowed it!

On Sunday
Jasper waited
and waited
and waited...

When Monday
came around again
he dug it up.

'That bean
will never make
a beanstalk,'
said Jasper.

But a   long,   long,

long   time   later...

It did!

(It was on a Thursday, I think.)

Now Jasper is looking for giants!

HODDER CHILDREN'S BOOKS

First published in Great Britain in 1992 by Hodder Children's Books
This edition published in 2016 by Hodder and Stoughton

10 9 8

Text and illustrations copyright © Nick Butterworth and Mick Inkpen, 1992

The moral rights of the author and illustrator have been asserted.

ISBN 978 1 444 91815 1

Printed in China

The paper and board used in this book are from wood from responsible sources.

MIX
Paper from
responsible sources
FSC® C104740

Hodder Children's Books
An imprint of
Hachette Children's Group
Part of Hodder and Stoughton
Carmelite House
50 Victoria Embankment
London EC4Y 0DZ

An Hachette UK Company
www.hachette.co.uk

www.hachettechildrens.co.uk